A Fishy Mystery

by Lisa Harkrader
Illustrated by Cary Pillo

The Kane Press
New York

For everyone who loves mysteries and dreams
of being a detective—L.H.

Thanks to dedicated school teachers, Tracy and Sally—C.P.

Acknowledgments: We wish to thank the following people for their helpful advice and review
of the material contained in this book: Susan Longo, Former Early Childhood and Elementary
School Teacher, Mamaroneck, NY; and Rebeka Eston Salemi, Kindergarten Teacher, Lincoln
School, Lincoln, MA.

Special thanks to Susan Longo and Meagan Branday Susi for providing the activities in the
back of this book.

Text copyright © 2017 by Lisa Harkrader
Illustrations copyright © 2017 by Cary Pillo

Library of Congress Cataloging-in-Publication Data

Names: Harkrader, Lisa, author. | Pillo, Cary, illustrator.
Title: A fishy mystery / by Lisa Harkrader ; iIllustrated by Cary Pillo.
Description: New York : Kane Press, [2017] | Series: Math matters | Summary:
    Junior detective Thea uses Venn diagrams to solve the case of the missing
    class goldfish.
Identifiers: LCCN 2016037416 (print) | LCCN 2016047815 (ebook) | ISBN
    9781575658667 (pbk. : alk. paper) | ISBN 9781575658698 (ebook)
Subjects: | CYAC: Venn diagrams—Fiction. | Schools—Fiction. | Mystery and
    detective stories.
Classification: LCC PZ7.H22615 Fi 2017 (print) | LCC PZ7.H22615 (ebook) | DDC
    [E]—dc23
LC record available at https://lccn.loc.gov/2016037416

10 9 8 7 6 5 4 3 2 1

First published in the United States of America in 2017 by Kane Press, Inc.
Printed in China

MATH MATTERS is a registered trademark of Kane Press, Inc.

Visit us online at www.kanepress.com

Like us on Facebook
facebook.com/kanepress

Follow us on Twitter
@kanepress

It was a dark and stormy morning the day the fish disappeared. I skidded into my classroom and dropped my backpack.

"Guess what I have," I said.

Austin and Zoe looked up.

"One of your birthday presents?" said Austin.

"A Sofia Sharp mystery?" said Zoe.

Austin and Zoe were my best friends. They knew me pretty well.

They also knew how to ruin a surprise.

"How'd you guess?" I said.

Austin shrugged. "It's the only thing you ever ask for, Thea."

He had a point. I loved reading Sofia Sharp
mysteries. Sofia was smart. She was brave.
With help from her two best friends, she
always cracked the case.

I knew I could be a detective like Sofia. I just
needed a case to solve.

"We got you a present, too," Austin said. "Only it's not a book."

"I think you'll like it anyway," said Zoe.

"Really?" I said. "What is it?"

But before they could answer . . . the bell rang.

"Good morning!" said Ms. Gruper.

Ms. Gruper was a good teacher. When she got going on math, even Rocky, our class goldfish, paid attention.

"Hold onto your hats," she said. "We're going to learn about—" Outside, thunder rumbled. "Venn diagrams! Now, who has a dog?"

Venn Diagrams

On the board, Ms. Gruper wrote the names of everyone who had a dog. Then she wrote down everyone who had a cat. Some kids had both.

She drew a rectangle. Inside that, she drew two circles that overlapped.

"In our class, we have a set of dog owners." She wrote the dog owners in one circle.

Dogs
Thea
Austin
Javier
Joanne
Cats
Ben
Malika
Penny
Both
Zoe
William
Edward

Venn Di
MS. GRUPER

Venn diagrams help you to organize information. Each circle contains a set of information. Start by labeling each circle. Then sort your data into the circles. Where the circles overlap—or **intersect**—you can see what the sets have in common!

"And a set of cat owners." She wrote the cat owners in the other circle.

"In the middle, the sets overlap." She wrote the dog and cat owners in the middle.

A girl named Charlotte waved her hand. "What if I don't have a pet?"

"Terrific question!" said Ms. Gruper. "If you're not in a set, you're still part of the diagram."

She wrote Charlotte's name in the rectangle outside both circles.

Charlotte nodded. But I could tell she didn't like being stuck in that rectangle.

Ms. Gruper turned us loose to make our own Venn diagrams.

Austin took to his like a dog takes to a T-bone steak. Zoe dove into hers, too.

I stared at mine. Then I had a brilliant idea. I started writing.

ROBOTS | ZOMBIES

beep a lot

might take over the planet

growl a lot

eat brains

don't eat food

AWESOME!!!

When I finished, I studied my diagram. In the middle, where the circles overlapped, was one word: girl.

I blinked. That was it? That was all I had in common with Sofia Sharp?

"You forgot something." Austin scribbled in the middle section. "Sofia has two best friends, and so do you."

As I gave him a fist bump, thunder rumbled and lightning flashed. The lights flickered.

The room went black.

Giggles filled the dark. We were used to this. At Larkspur Elementary, the lights went out every time it stormed.

Then I heard something new: footsteps, and a clank.

I always carried an emergency case-cracking kit. I pulled out my flashlight. As I flicked it on, I saw a shape dart through the darkness.

Lightning flashed again, and the lights
buzzed back on. Everyone giggled in relief.
Then I heard a gasp. I looked up.

Zoe was pointing to the bookshelf where Rocky's fish bowl always sat.

The shelf was empty.

"Oh, no!"

"Where's Rocky?"

The room erupted in chatter. Ms. Gruper tried to calm everyone down. We searched the classroom . . . but Rocky was gone.

I opened my kit. "We have to solve this," I told Austin and Zoe. "Rocky needs us."

We dusted the scene for prints. But too many jumbled fingerprints covered the room.

"Our custodian's at a floor polishing convention," Ms. Gruper told us. "He hasn't been here to clean."

We found water spilled on the bookshelf.
Austin sniffed it. "Smells fishy," he said.

We collected evidence from Rocky's bookshelf:
a rubber band, some fish food flakes, and a
chewed-up pencil. I didn't think any of it would
lead us to Rocky. But we bagged it anyway.

I recorded all the clues in my detective notebook.

After a thorough investigation, I said, "Rocky isn't here. And nobody left the room. Maybe the culprit came in from the hallway."

At recess, we questioned kids in other classes. Did any students leave their rooms? Any teachers? The principal?

But nobody had been lurking about.

I flipped through my pages of clues. I had to find the answer. There was a missing fish out there, and he needed me.

"I know!" I slapped my forehead. "Mr. Olsen!"

"Our custodian?" said Austin. "But he's so nice. And he loves Rocky."

I nodded. "Exactly. He loves Rocky, *and* he's always in the halls. What if he wanted Rocky for himself?"

I climbed up on a bench so everyone could hear me.

"I've cracked the case," I announced. "The fish thief is—"

"Uh, Thea?" Zoe shook my arm.

Austin pointed to a page in my notebook.
"Mr. Olsen was at a floor polishing convention."

I stared at the page. I couldn't believe it. Mr. Olsen's alibi was right there, in all those pages of evidence.

And I'd missed it.

I slumped onto the bench. I wasn't like Sofia
Sharp. I couldn't even keep my clues straight.
I'd never be a detective.

Someone squeezed my shoulder. I looked up.

"You know," said Ms. Gruper, "Venn diagrams aren't just for math. They can solve real problems, too. Even mysteries."

I thought about this. She was right. My clues needed to be organized. "Thanks, Ms. G!" I said.

When the whistle blew, I marched back inside.

Sofia Sharp says a culprit needs two things to commit a crime: a CHANCE to do it and a REASON to do it. I drew two circles.

In one circle, I wrote down everyone who sat close enough to the fish bowl to grab it while the lights were out. In the other circle, I wrote down anyone who had a reason to take Rocky.

I knew the middle, where the circles overlapped, would give me the answer.

But the middle was empty.

Charlotte wanted a pet. But she didn't sit near Rocky. Mr. Olsen was out of town. Who else had a reason?

Austin and Zoe sat the closest. But they wouldn't take a fish.

Unless . . .

I stared at my two best friends. A smile spread over my face.

"It was *you*!" I said. "You sit closest to the fish bowl. You said you had a gift for me. And all I ever ask for is—"

"A mystery!" said Austin. "And you solved it."

Zoe grinned. "Happy birthday!"

I sat back in my chair, letting the wonder of it sink in. I *did* solve it. I solved a real-life mystery, just like Sofia Sharp.

Except . . .

"Where's Rocky?" I said.

Ms. Gruper unlocked her filing cabinet and, with a flourish, lifted out the fish bowl. Rocky swam happily inside.

"You can't pull a caper in my classroom without me," she said.

Austin nodded. "Ms. Gruper was in on it. She wanted us to get excited about Venn diagrams."

I *was* excited. I was so excited, I started drawing circles—three this time.

"We have another case to crack," I said. "I have a birthday party coming up, and we need to track down the perfect cake!"

CAKE FLAVORS WE LOVE!

THEA

AUSTIN

red velvet
raspberry
mint chip

marble
pecan

vanilla
lemon
cherry

chocolate

carrot
pineapple

fudge
strawberry

banana
coconut
pumpkin

ZOE

Happy Birthday Thea

VENN DIAGRAMS

Venn facts!
- Venn diagrams give us lots of information.
- Venn diagrams organize sets (a set is collection of things).
- Venn diagrams help show how things may be similar or different.

How to sort the following set of shapes using a Venn diagram:

1. Draw two overlapping circles and label them according to how you want to sort the shapes—for example, **blue** and **square**.
2. If a shape is blue but not square, put it in the circle labeled **blue**.
3. If a shape is square but not blue, put it in the circle labeled **square**.
4. If a shape is blue *and* square, put it in the middle section where the circles overlap. (Note: Not every shape in the set may belong in one of the circles.)

Now you have a Venn diagram!

Bonus: You can make a three-part Venn diagram using the same set of shapes!

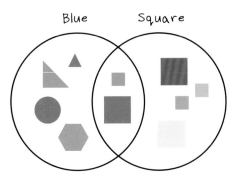

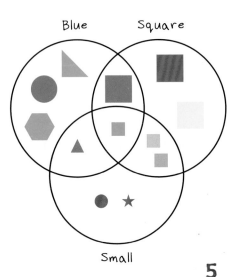